It Must

HURT

A Lot

A book about
death
and learning
and growing

the story by
Doris Sanford

& pictures by
Graci Evans

© 1986 by Multnomah Press
Portland, Oregon 97266
Printed in Hong Kong
All Rights reserved.
90 91 – 10 9 8 7 6 5
ISBN 0-88070-131-5

Sanford, Doris.
  It must hurt a lot.
  Cover title.
  Summary: Describes a boy's reactions of
anger, grief, and eventual acceptance when
his dog dies. Includes suggestions to parents
for helping a child deal with loss.
  1. Death—Juvenile literature. 2. Grief—
Juvenile literature. 3. Loss (Psychology)—
Juvenile literature. [1. Death] I. Evans, Graci,
ill.   II. Title.
HQ1073.3.S26   1985   155.9'37   86-25009
ISBN 0-88070-131-5

to Anya

a tiny friend
with a

GIANT

LOSS

JOSHUA
knew something
was wrong
when he came
in the door.

Mom said, "I have something to tell you", and she wasn't smiling. As a matter of fact her voice was sad and Joshua thought she would cry. Then she said it…

"Muffin was hit by a car this morning and

SHE DIED!!!"

Mom
put her
arms
around
him and
they both
cried hard.

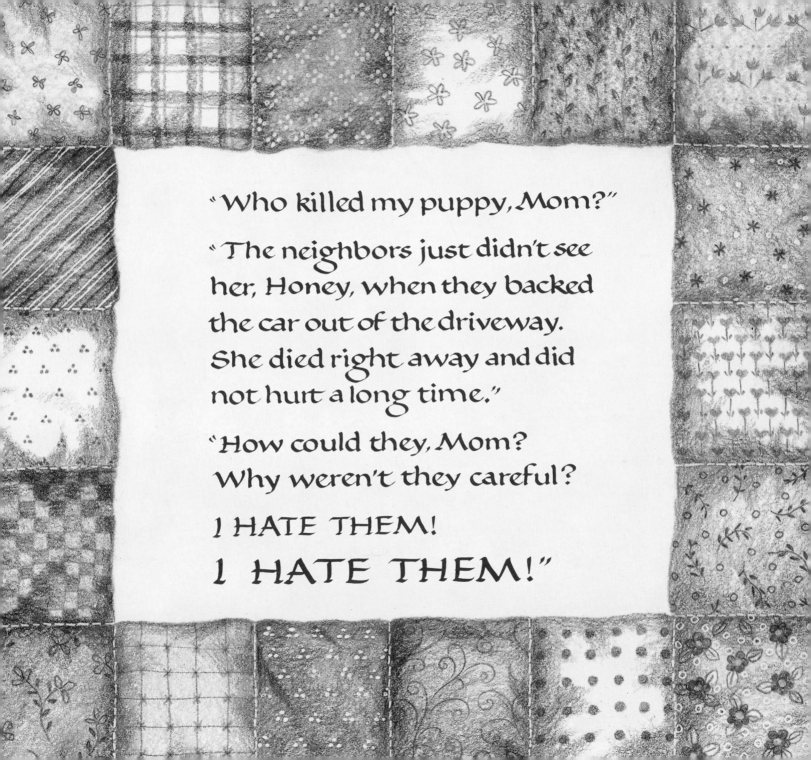

"Who killed my puppy, Mom?"

"The neighbors just didn't see
her, Honey, when they backed
the car out of the driveway.
She died right away and did
not hurt a long time."

"How could they, Mom?
Why weren't they careful?

I HATE THEM!

I HATE THEM!"

Joshua wanted to be alone.
He had never hurt so much
in his WHOLE LIFE!
Muffin was his very best
friend. She slept on Joshua's
bed, licked his tears, played
ball, and waited by Joshua's
plate every night at dinner

because Joshua was
the messiest eater
of all...

sometimes on purpose!

Mom said he could get
another puppy, but he
didn't WANT another
puppy. He wanted
                    Muffin.

DIDN'T ANYBODY
UNDERSTAND?

The next day Tim came over.
Tim was Joshua's friend and
they loved to play together,
but today was different.
Tim acted funny and he
**NEVER MENTIONED
MUFFIN!**

Not once!

Joshua knew he had been
told. Pretty soon Tim said,
"Well, I have to go home now."

And he did.

For weeks it was awful! Sometimes Joshua would forget about Muffin for a little while, then when he remembered, it hurt so much. At night he ALWAYS cried himself to sleep. It felt like his whole world had been taken away.

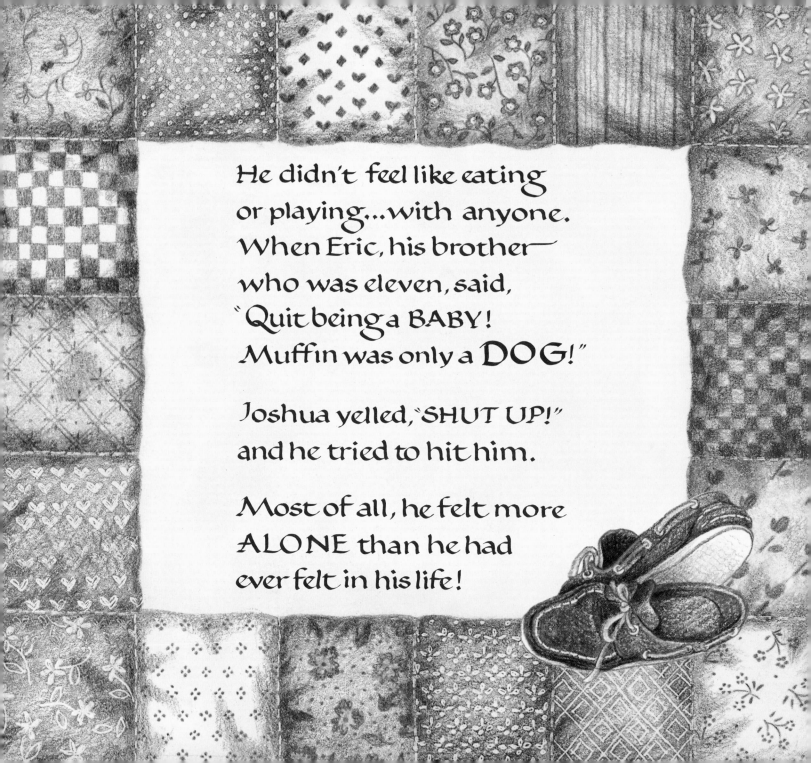

He didn't feel like eating
or playing...with anyone.
When Eric, his brother
who was eleven, said,
"Quit being a BABY!
Muffin was only a DOG!"

Joshua yelled, "SHUT UP!"
and he tried to hit him.

Most of all, he felt more
ALONE than he had
ever felt in his life!

It didn't happen right away,
but one day when Joshua
was thinking hard
all by himself,
he knew that
some **BIG**
changes were
happening
inside
him.

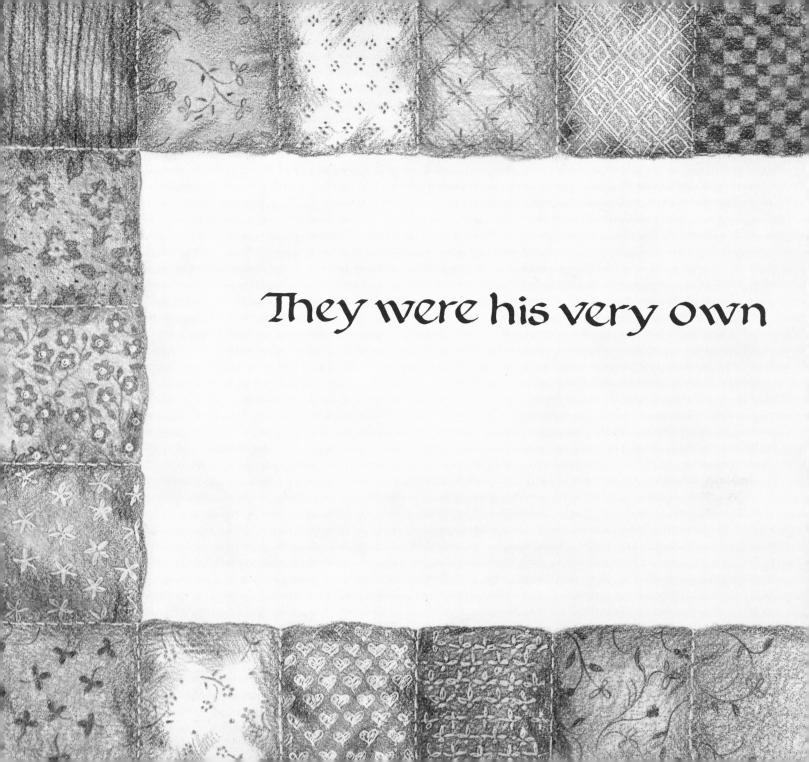

They were his very own

SPECIAL SECRETS

but he said I could tell just you...

When Mom wanted to
get another puppy right
away, she just wanted to
FIX everything because
she loved Joshua so much.

But it was Muffin that
Joshua missed.

so the first secret is...

When I love
lots I hurt
lots.

MUFFIN

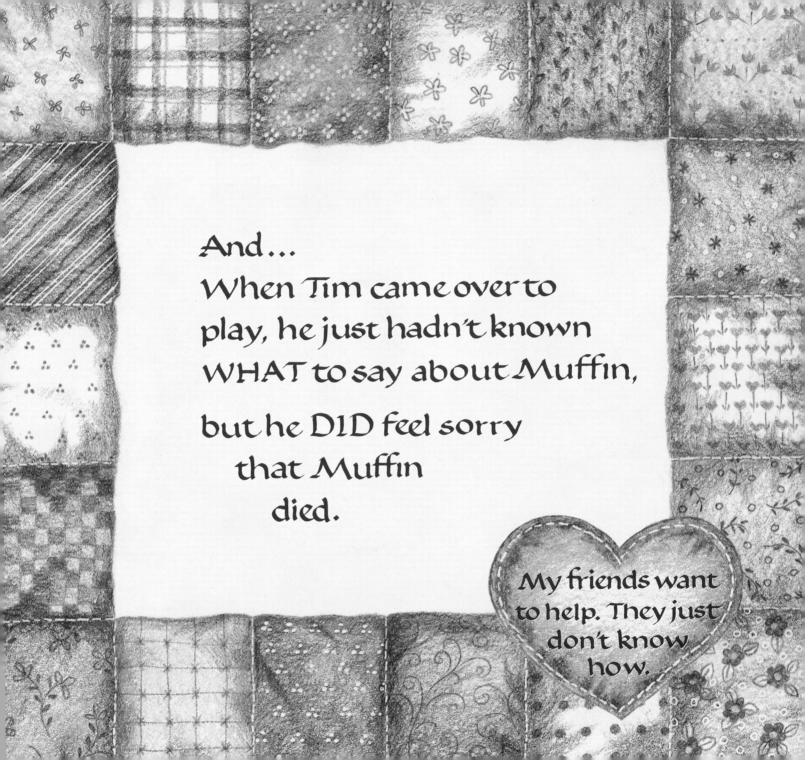

And …
When Tim came over to
play, he just hadn't known
WHAT to say about Muffin,

but he DID feel sorry
   that Muffin
      died.

My friends want
to help. They just
   don't know
      how.

When Eric yelled at Joshua for crying, it was because HE was near tears himself!

He loved Muffin, too.
He just acted
differently.

Everybody
handles feelings
in his own
way.

Joshua was SO glad he
TOLD Muffin how much
he loved her and had
kissed her on her cold,
wet nose every day. It
would be awful if MUFFIN
had died not knowing how
much Joshua loved her.

If you love
somebody
tell him
NOW.

A month later when Tim's Grandma died, Joshua sat on Tim's bed and cried. (Not JUST because she made the best chocolate chip cookies of anybody, but because Joshua knew how it felt to lose someone you love.)

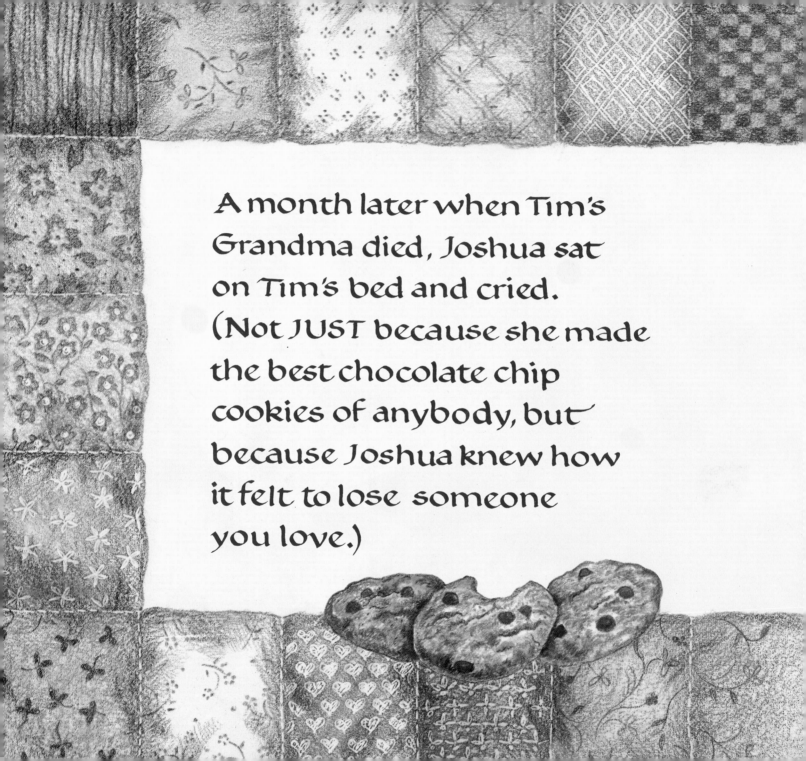

I can help
my friends
when they
hurt.

In time Joshua DID begin to feel better. He thought about all the fun times with Muffin, and he was glad they had been best friends. He was stronger now, and Muffin's death had helped him grow.

GOOD
memories
always
stay.

All these secrets warmed Joshua.

HOW TO HELP A CHILD WITH LOSS

Dear Friend,

ALL CHILDREN EXPERIENCE LOSS! Loss is a part of growing up. Although loss always hurts, even a young child can learn that beautiful surprises come wrapped in the "package" of loss. We encourage you to talk about these gifts. SENSITIVE, CARING ADULTS ARE MADE, NOT BORN.

1. Talk about loss whenever the child asks questions.
2. Answer honestly and only what's asked.
3. Don't use philosophical terms, use plain English.
4. Remember, until they are about nine years old, most children don't understand that death is permanent.
5. Tell the child he did not cause a death by his anger. (Children confuse the wish with the deed.)